Text copyright © 2017 by Mac Barnett
Illustrations copyright © 2017 by Brian Biggs
Published by Roaring Brook Press
Roaring Brook Press is a division of Holtzbrinck
Publishing Holdings Limited Partnership
175 Fifth Avenue, New York, New York 10010
mackids.com

Library of Congress Cataloging-in-Publication Data

Names: Barnett, Mac, author. | Biggs, Brian, illustrator.
Title: Noisy night / Mac Barnett ; illustrated by Brian Biggs.
Description: First edition. | New York : Roaring Brook Press, 2016. |
    Summary: "A clever picture book about a multi-level apartment
    building's occupants and their many nighttime noises"— Provided
    by publisher.
Identifiers: LCCN 2016002016 | ISBN 9781596439672 (hardback)
Subjects: | CYAC: Picture books. | Night—Fiction. | Bedtime—
    Fiction. | Apartment houses—Fiction. | BISAC: JUVENILE FICTION
    / Humorous Stories. | JUVENILE FICTION / Bedtime & Dreams.
Classification: LCC PZ7.B26615 No 2016 | DDC [E]—dc23
LC record available at https://lccn.loc.gov/2016002016

Our books may be purchased in bulk for promotional,
educational, or business use. Please contact your local bookseller
or the Macmillan Corporate and Premium Sales Department
at (800) 221-7945 ext. 5442 or by e-mail at
MacmillanSpecialMarkets@macmillan.com.

First edition 2017
Printed in China by Toppan Leefung Printing Ltd.,
Dongguan City, Guangdong Province

10 9 8 7 6 5 4 3 2 1

NOISY NIGHT

by
MAC BARNETT

pictures by
BRIAN BIGGS

Roaring Brook Press/ New York

Cowboys are laughing
above my head.

A CROW IS SQUAWKING ABOVE MY HEAD.

A sheep is speaking above my head.

what is going **BAA BAA BAA** above my head?

A baby is cooing
above my head.

CHEERLEADERS ARE CHEERING
ABOVE MY HEAD.

An old man
is hollering...